Why Do I Have to Eat Off the Floor?

Chris Hornsey ❖ *Illustrations by* Gwyn Perkins

WALKER & COMPANY ☀ NEW YORK

Why can't I drive the car?

Because you are too small to drive.

Why can't I dig in the garden?

Because we want the flowers to grow.

Why do I have to take a bath after playing in the mud?

Because you should be clean when you are inside.

Why can't I sleep in your bed?

Because you have your own bed.

Why can't we play ALL the time?

Because there are other things we have to do.

Why can't I have a pet duck or an elephant?

Because you wouldn't be able to take care of them.

Why do I have to be good when we have company?

Because we want them to see how well-behaved you are.

Why can't I jump on the chair?

Because chairs are for sitting.

But . . .

why do I have to eat off the floor?

Because . . . you are a DOG, Murphy! D-O-G!

Dogs can't drive cars, and dogs shouldn't dig in gardens,
and dogs must have baths, and dogs should sleep in their own beds,
and dogs can't have pets, and dogs shouldn't jump on chairs,
and dogs eat off the floor!

Dogs are *dogs*, Murphy, and they should always be good.

For Thomas, and in memory of Hazel
—C. H.

For Marie, Georgia, and Hubert
—G. P.

First published in the United States of America in 2007 by
Walker Publishing Company, Inc.
Distributed to the trade by Holtzbrinck Publishers
First published in Australia in 2005 by Little Hare Books

For information about permission to reproduce selections from
this book, write to Permissions, Walker & Company,
104 Fifth Avenue, New York, New York 10011

Library of Congress Cataloging-in-Publication Data available upon request
ISBN-10: 0-8027-9617-6 • ISBN-13: 978-0-8027-9617-2 (hardcover)

Visit Walker & Company's Web site at www.walkeryoungreaders.com

Produced by Phoenix Offset, Hong Kong
Printed in China

2 4 6 8 10 9 7 5 3 1